For Adam, my parents and anyone who feels like Keith

First published in 2019 by Child's Play (International) Ltd
Ashworth Road, Bridgemead, Swindon SN5 7YD, UK

First published in USA in 2020 by Child's Play Inc
250 Minot Avenue, Auburn, Maine 04210

Distributed in Australia by Child's Play Australia Pty Ltd
Unit 10/20 Narabang Way, Belrose, Sydney, NSW 2085

ISBN 978-1-78628-343-6
CLP020719CPL08193436

Printed in Shenzhen, China

1 3 5 7 9 10 8 6 4 2

A catalogue record of this book
is available from the British Library

www.childs-play.com

Keith among the PIGEONS

GIVE PIGEONS
A CHANCE

Katie Brosnan

This is Keith.

Just like all cats,
Keith loves to
take a nap,

make himself nice and clean...

But Nigel and Hilda weren't sure about Keith.

I much prefer
pigeons, anyway,
thought Keith.

Keith wanted to get to know them better.

But every time he
got close enough
to say hello...

they made a swift exit.

Oh poo!

I just need to be a bit more pigeon, thought Keith.

me-cooo
me-coo
coo coo

So he tried and tried...

everything he could get his paws on.

KEITH

But after all his efforts,
Keith still wasn't very pigeon.

Then he had an idea!

Now I am a
PIGEON!

I just need to work
on my landing!

But then it started to rain...

and that's when
everyone saw Keith
wasn't a pigeon at all.

Well, if Keith really had to be a cat...
he would try to be
a proper one.

But nothing about being a proper cat felt right.

The next morning Keith got up early.